MW00768428

Your Mommy Was Just Like You

By Kelly Bennett Illustrated by David Walker

G. P. Putnam's Sons • An Imprint of Penguin Group (USA) Inc.

G. P. PUTNAM'S SONS
A division of Penguin Young Readers Group. Published by The Penguin Group. Penguin Group (USA) Inc., 375 Hudson Street, New York, NY 10014, U.S.A. Penguin Group (Canada), 90 Eglinton Avenue East, Suite 700, Toronto, Ontario M4P 2Y3, Canada (a division of Pearson Penguin Canada Inc.). Penguin Books Ltd, 80 Strand, London WC2R ORL, England. Penguin Ireland, 25 St. Stephen's Green, Dublin 2, Ireland (a division of Penguin Books Ltd.). Penguin Group (Australia), 250 Camberwell Road, Camberwell, Victoria 3124, Australia (a division of Pearson Australia Group Pty Ltd). Penguin Books India Pvt Ltd, 11 Community Centre, Panchsheel Park, New Delhi - 110 017, India. Penguin Group (NZ), 67 Apollo Drive, Rosedale, North Shore 0632, New Zealand (a division of Pearson New Zealand Ltd). Penguin Books (South Africa) (Pty) Ltd, 24 Sturdee Avenue, Rosebank, Johannesburg 2196, South Africa. Penguin Books Ltd, Registered Offices: 80 Strand, London WC2R ORL, England.

Design by Richard Amari.
Text set in Sinclair Medium Script.
The art was created using layers of acrylic paints on paper.

Library of Congress Cataloging-in-Publication Data
Bennett, Kelly. Your mommy was just like you / Kelly Bennett ; illustrated by David Walker. p. cm. Summary: A grandmother describes to her granddaughter how her mother was just like her as a child, playing peekaboo, getting sent to time-out, and collecting crazy things. [1. Mothers and daughters—Fiction. 2. Behavior—Fiction. 3. Grandmothers—Fiction.] I. Walker, David, 1965– ill. II. Title. PZ7.B4425You 2011 [E]—dc22 2009032101

ISBN 978-0-399-24798-9
1 3 5 7 9 10 8 6 4 2

For Alexis Rose,
forever my baby.

And a huge hug to Ellen Yeomans,
whose sharp eye and soft touch made
the difference!

K.B.

For Mia Louise,
and her mom.

D.W.

Your mommy

was born bright-eyed and fuzzy-topped.

Just like you.

I'd rock her and
blow on her tummy
and tickle her toes.

She'd giggle and coo, and play
"Where's Baby Peek-a-boo?"
Just like you.

Your mommy had a special friend
named Whiney Baby.
Whiney had clumpy hair,
and her face was smooshed.
But that never mattered to your mommy.

"Want to go for a ride?"
asked Uncle John.
"Whiney, too!" said your mommy.
Just like you.

Most days your mommy was my
sweet potato—doll face—poopsie.

But some days
she turned into
THE TERROR!

She pestered and poked,
stomped and spit,
or threw herself on the floor, kicking and
hollering, "NO, NO, NO!"

On those days
she was sent to
TIME-OUT.
Just like you.

Your mommy was bouncy
and twirly-whirly.
Just like you.
She loved to play games,
but she didn't always win.

Sometimes she got hurt.
I'd bandage her scrapes
and give her extra lovies.
After, she always
wanted to play again.

At times your
mommy was a frog,

or a robot.

Then she was
a magic fairy,

or a beautiful princess.

Sometimes I mistook her
for a famous inventor.

Your mommy never
wanted her hair brushed
or her face washed.
And she insisted on
choosing her own outfits.

She primped and
spangled
and made herself
kooky costumes.
Just like you.

Your mommy collected lots of stuff, just like you.

And she loved to build things with it, like

sculptures,

daisy chains,

dollhouses,

and hideouts with signs saying TOP SECRET.

When she started school,
your mommy was still
learning to tie her shoes,

ride a two-wheeler,

and blow bubbles.

She didn't know how to read or write
or count to a million zillion, either.
But your mommy learned,
and practiced,
and kept getting smarter
and smarter and smarter.
Just like you.

dog
cat
pig

Your mommy was never ready
for lights-out.
First, her baby had to be tucked in
and all her animals
had to be hugged good night.

I'd say, "Sweet dreams, sweetie pie."
She'd say, "Read one more story?
A short one? Pleeease?"
Just like you.

Every morning, when your mommy woke up,
I gave her a cuddle and kiss.
And said a prayer of thanks that she was mine.

Your mommy is my baby.
And no matter how big she gets,
or how old she gets,
she will always be my baby.

Just like you.